# Come away from the water, Shirley

## John Burningham

Jonathan Cape, London

*By the same author*
TIME TO GET OUT OF THE BATH, SHIRLEY

First published 1977
1 3 5 7 9 10 8 6 4 2
© John Burningham 1977
John Burningham has asserted his right under
the Copyright, Designs and Patents Act 1988
to be identified as the author of this work
First published in the United Kingdom in 1977 by
Jonathan Cape Limited
Random House, 20 Vauxhall Bridge Road, London SW1V 2SA
Reprinted 1983, 1986, 1991, 1993
Random House UK Limited Reg. No. 954009
ISBN 0 224 01373 4
Printed in China

# Of course it's far too cold for swimming, Shirley

# We are going to put our chairs up here

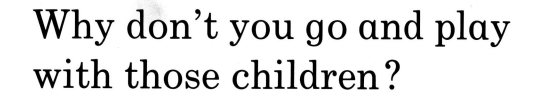

Why don't you go and play
with those children?

Mind you don't get any of that filthy tar
on your nice new shoes

Don't stroke that dog, Shirley,
you don't know where he's been

That's the third and last time I'm asking you whether you want a drink, Shirley

Careful where you're throwing those stones.
You might hit someone.

You won't bring any of that
smelly seaweed home, will you, Shirley

Your father might have a game with you
when he's had a little rest

# We ought to be getting back soon

Good heavens! Just look at the time.
We are going to be late if we don't hurry.

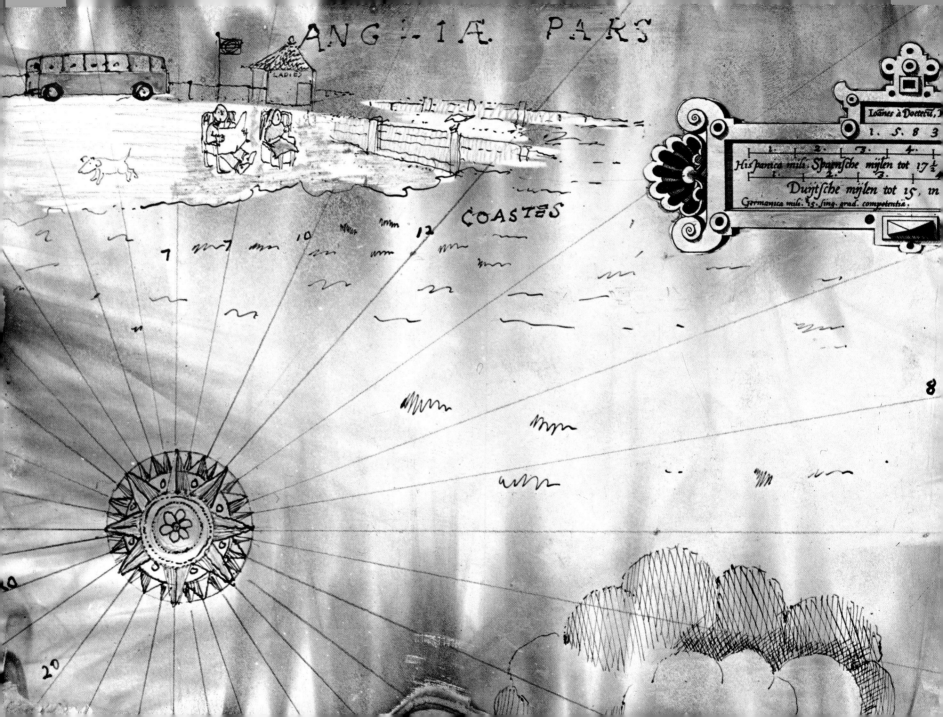

ANGLIÆ PARS

COASTES

Ioānes à Doetecū

1. 5. 83

Hispanica mili. Spaensche mijlen tot 17½

Duytsche mijlen tot 15. m

Germanica mili. 15. sing. grad. compotentia.